Scram!

CANDLEWICK PRESS

The Story
of How We Got
Our Dog

Lauren Child

For Trisha, of course

Nothing ever happens
except for sometimes . . .
And only on rare-ish occasions,
which is hardly ever.

I mainly always find *something* to do even if
there is nothing going on, which might be cutting
things up and turning them into something else.
I can do this for a long time unless my younger
brother comes into my room, which is also his.

I don't like sharing a room because it means
someone has permission to disturb you even
when you are minding your own business and
are alone-ly happy.

If I read, then it will be in the linen closet.
It's warm in there with all the towels and sheets
and it's dark
unless you have a flashlight,
which I do.

Although it doesn't always light up, because my
sister, Marcie, usually unscrews the end and steals
the batteries out.

If there is absolutely nothing else to do, then I
am very good at staring out the window. It is
a way of noticing things by accident, which is
almost always more interesting than noticing
them on purpose.

And it is how for example e.g. you one day
watch a camel walking down the road when it
really *shouldn't*,

       because camels don't exist

              in Navarino Street.

Navarino Street is our street and the houses are all joined together at the sides and they slope downward in a curve. Seven of us live in our house and one of us is Grandad, who has a room on the first floor, because he can be wobbly on the stairs. I have an older brother named Kurt and a younger brother named Minal Cricket and an older sister named Marcie, who steals batteries out of other people's flashlights. Other than that my family is my mom and my dad and me, Clarice Bean. We have a cat *sometimes* but he spends a lot of the day eating food at other people's houses and cannot be relied on to be a pet when you need him.

Luckily our cat, Fuzzy, does not eat birds or he would have to move out for always because you see Grandad is very attached to birds and does not like them being eaten by cats.

Grandad has his own bird who is a canary named Chirp. Chirp is one of Grandad's best friends. He lets her fly around his room and sing on his shoulder.

Chirp is Grandad's always-there companion. Grandad likes company but he says he doesn't always need to talk.

He says, "Sometimes I just want to sit with somebody and be understood without words."

Chirp is good for this because she doesn't know any words—she only does tunes—and Grandad says, "You can float away on a good tune, and floating away is sometimes just the ticket."

I am in agreement with Grandad, except for the part about not needing to talk.

I *always* need to talk, but I often wish there was more listening and less talking back.

So it seems very unfair that I have to share a room with Minal Cricket.

He does nothing *but* not listening.

Someone who is a good listener is my granny. She is also a good talker. She knows everything and when she doesn't she comes up with something. She says she's good at figuring things out. That's her talent.

I am often wondering what mine is.

Granny lives in New York, and we have long conversations on the telephone.

She says I am one of those people who is good at finding the interesting. She says, "People who find the interesting *are* interesting."

She says, "You are a very resourceful person, Clarice Bean." She means I am good at coming up with ideas when there aren't any.

So maybe *that* is my talent.

But there are some times when even I can't turn the **nothing** into more than it is.

I hate the nothing days.

When the day feels nothingy, I tend to lie on the floor and wish I wasn't lying on the floor.

It's very hard to get up when you feel like this.

But there's **nothing**
you can do about it.

When things start nothingy, they always get more and more nothing until someone throws someone else's duvet out the window or pinches someone else on the arm and the someone else tells Mom.

Pinching is not allowed.

Everyone gets angry and fed up on the nothing days but it just can't be helped.

It's no one's fault, and in the end the only thing to do is go to bed at bedtime and cross your toes that you will wake up differently.

But there was one day in the summer that began as a nothing day
and then everything happened.

Absolutely
almost
everything.

It started like this . . .

I am sitting on the counter and Mom is trying to edge a wasp out the window, which she can't get open because it got painted into stuck.

She says, "Clarice Bean, why don't you go and *do* something?"

And I say, "I'm trying to think what to do but there's nothing."

Mom says, "NOTHING? Really? Nothing?"

I say, "Exactly. Nothing."

Mom says, "How can there be nothing to do? There's *always* something to do."

I say, "Because today is the same as yesterday."

And she says, "But you didn't complain about

having **nothing to do** *then*."

And I say, "No, that's because it was different but today it's the same."

She says, "It is the very first week of the summer vacation. Are you really going to be like this until you go back to school?"

I say, "It's just the weather. It's weighing me down with hotness."

She says, "If it was raining, you would be complaining about that."

I say, "Yes, but the hotness is worse because it is interfering with my brain so I can't think of ideas, which means there's nothing to do."

And she says, "Well, *I* can give you something to do, if you're so stuck for ideas: you can pack up the rest of the pantry. All the food has to go into boxes."

And I say, "Why?"

And she says, "Because I am putting up new shelves."

And I say, "Why?"

And she says, "Because we need more space for food."

And I say, "Why?"

And she says, "Because I have four children who never stop eating."

And I say, "Can I have a cookie?"

And she says, "Your brother ate them all."

And I say, "That's so unfair."

And she says, "If you actually *did* something, it would take your mind off the unfairness."

I say, "But that's the problem. I can't think of what."

Mom says, "For goodness' sake, Clarice Bean, you are sending me cuckoo with all your nothing-to-do!"

I say, "It's not my fault."

And she says, "Will you just go outside!"

And I say, "I can't be bothered."

And she says,

"Scram!"

It's times like this that I would normally phone Betty Moody.

Betty Moody is my best friend and I am hers, so we mainly like doing everything together. But she has gone off on vacation the minute school ended. Her family will be away for the whole entire summer because they are lucky.

And I am stuck with being on my own outside in the backyard.

Of course Robert Granger is sitting on the wall pretending to be an orangutan.

He is always pretending to be something.

If you could see him, you would know what I mean.

He has on a very fluffy orangutan-colored sweater—even though it is squelching hot—and he is pretending to eat bugs off it like you would do if you were

an actual orangutan

but he is just a pretend one.

As soon as he sees me, he says,

"Guess what," in a loud voice.

He only talks in LOUD.

I don't bother to guess because he's going to tell me anyway.

He says,

"I've got a rabbit."

I say, "You have a rabbit?"

He says,

"It's borrowed from my cousin."

I say, "So it's NOT your rabbit."

He says, "It is . . .

until September."

I am speechless with envy.

He says, "Do you want to see it?"

The thing is, I do actually want to see the borrowed rabbit. But it's also a trap—that's what **Ruby Redfort** would say. **Ruby Redfort** is a girl in a book who is an expert in everything and a secret agent and she knows how to avoid tricky situations that can lead into danger.

In this case the danger is boredom because you can bet yourself that as soon as you get over the wall Robert Granger won't let you even hold his borrowed rabbit but he will keep on talking and talking until you actually are feeling so dreary that you can't climb back into safety.

So I say, "I haven't got time to see your borrowed rabbit because I'm very busy doing things."

He says, "What things are you doing?"

And I say, "Stuff."

And he says, "What stuff?"

And I say, "Stuff stuff."

And he says, "If you were doing stuff, you'd tell me what it was."

This is actually NOT true because I try never to tell Robert Granger ever what I am up to.

But this time I do because I am angry that he has a borrowed rabbit and I don't, so I say,

"We are also getting a pet.
Maybe an actual rabbit,
or a tortoise, or . . ."

I am trying to think of what else we might
pretend to get and I almost say horse, but then
I remember the pet Marcie is desperate for,
and I say,

"Or a dog."

He is speechless.

Which I am not surprised about.

He says, "Really?"

And I say,

"Completely actually.
But we won't have to give it back
in September because it
won't be borrowed."

And he says,

"I don't believe you."

Which is typical of Robert Granger.

Why can't he ever believe you?

And I say,
"Well, you might as well
because it's true."

And he says,
"I'm sorry, but I don't
have **time** to talk
to **you** because I need
to **check** on an
actual existing **rabbit**."

And then he slides down from the wall and buzzes away.

I just can't believe that even Robert Granger is luckier than me. He might have only a *borrowed* rabbit but I don't even have a made-up one.

Marcie's soccer ball is lying in the flower bed, so I kick it very hard at the fence and I must be a good kicker because it goes straight through the wood into Mrs. Stampney's yard.

There is no way I am going to ask for it back because Mrs. Stampney is a crab apple and does not take sorry for an answer even with a box of Jelly Fruits.

One thing I have learned is the best thing to do in this situation is pretend it never happened.

So I cover up the hole in the fence by pulling the creeping plant down over it.

I hope it won't be found.

There is nothing to do inside either
                and I can't even sit in the linen

closet because it is too hot.

And I can't even sit in my *bedroom* closet because the light bulb has stopped lighting up. And my emergency flashlight is not working because my sister, Marcie, has stolen the batteries again. She uses them in her radio, which is never not on, and so I am always usually left with a flashlight that doesn't light up.

Not lighting up is pointless when it comes to flashlights.

I am thinking of saving up for one of those windup ones that doesn't require any extra powering. They don't cost too much compared to some things, but they cost a *lot* to someone who is already saving up $5 for something much more rarer than a windup flashlight.

I tiptoe around in socks to see if I can find any other batteries without going into the kitchen, which is when I remember that the television remote controller takes two,

and two is exactly how many I need.

I fish them out and go back to my room to find my comics.

I keep them under my bed with a china pig standing on them. But the pig is standing on nothing. And the comics are not there. And I know it must be my sister who took them.

I storm into Marcie's room, which is absolutely not allowed but luckily she is at Casey's, so she will never know.

I have to be careful because if I get on Marcie's bad side then saving up the $5 will all be for nothing.

You see, the thing I most want in the whole entire world is Marcie's **rainbow roller skates**, which she has grown out of.

I have wanted these skates ever since Marcie got them for her birthday millions of years ago.

They have loopy laces and **rainbows** swooping on the sides and I have been waiting to grow into them since I first saw them.

Every time I almost reach $5 in my piggy bank,

something happens and I have to spend some of it on e.g. the grab bag at school or an emergency bag of chips.

At the moment I only have $3.79.

I am hoping my sister won't sell them to someone else before I have saved up the whole amount.

So you can see why I have to be unnoticed. In this type of situation, **Ruby Redfort** would say,

"Whatever you DO, you MUST cover your TRACKS."

Ruby is good at covering her tracks because she has to be undercover and if anyone ever finds out what she is up to then she won't be undercover anymore.

I search around but it turns out my comics aren't in Marcie's room. They aren't anywhere.

And that's when I remember.

I took them all to Betty Moody's because we

wanted to read them on her beanbags.

But of course Betty is away for the summer. This means I will not have my comics for at least ages.

Since I am already in Marcie's room, I decide I might as well check to see if she has any other interesting things to read. But all her magazines are about hairstyles and eyelashes and I am not interested in those subjects.

I am about to tiptoe out when I notice a very shiny magazine sticking out from under her bed. It's brand-new and it's called

There's Nothing Like a ... DOG.

There is a dog in a beret and the words:

IS YOUR DOG SPEAKING YOUR LANGUAGE?

A FREE pull-out guide on how to speak DOG.

There's also a FREE gift attached, which is flip-flops with a dog-bone design on the underneath. I peel them off the cover and try them on.

They are quite large.

It doesn't surprise me that my sister has this magazine because she is DESPERATE for a dog and most of her posters are of dogs, and if they aren't they are of smiling boys with odd hairstyles. The magazine looks interesting,

so I flump down and start reading. It turns out that it's true:

there *is* nothing like a dog

except for some sorts of cats and also pigs who have the same loyalness and who you can train to be exactly almost like a dog. It is fascinating and at the same time very interesting

and also very hot in Marcie's room.

It's hard

to keep

my eyes

open.

I fall asleep
with my face
crumpled
on a picture
of a
beagle.

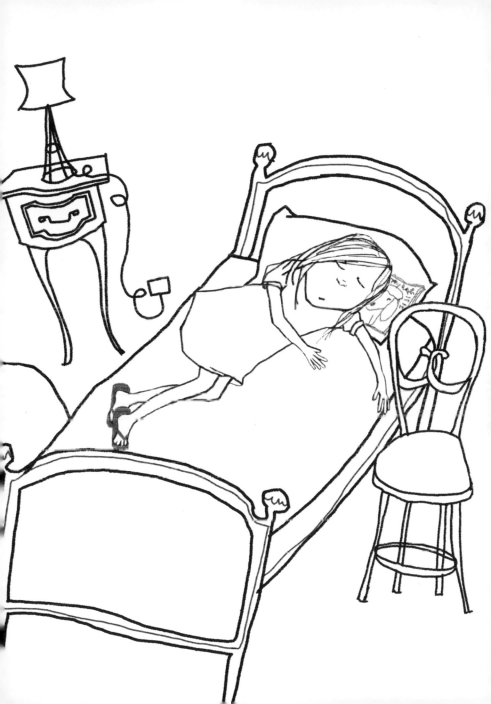

I am disturbed into being awake by an angry sound from downstairs.

Which is a voice saying,

"COULD YOU POSSIBLY EXPLAIN WHAT AN ORANGE *SOCCER BALL* IS DOING IN MY BIRDBATH?"

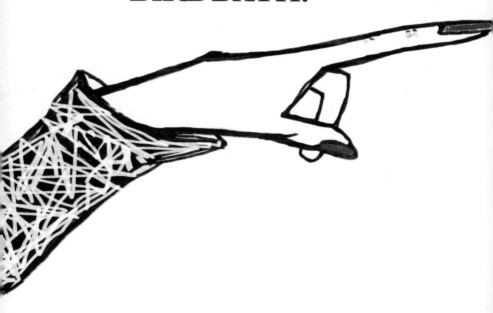

Mom is saying,

"I'm sorry, Mrs. Stampney.

I've told her so many times . . .

Marcie!"

But of course there is no answer because Marcie is out somewhere else.

Mom starts calling for Grandad because she knows he is the only one Mrs. Stampney is never rude to. If he appears, she will have to pipe down. Mrs. Stampney wouldn't dare shout at Grandad.

Kurt calls out, "Grandad's gone to Peggy's." Peggy is Grandad's best friend and she lives in the neighborhood not that far away but even Mrs. Stampney's loud voice won't reach all the way to Peggy's house. So Grandad won't know to come to the rescue.

There is lots more complaining until the moaning is shuffled out and goes back next door. I can hear her muttering, "Those children are completely irresponsible."

When I'm sure Mrs. Stampney is not going to march back, I creep downstairs and keep a lowish profile.

Mom is happy to see me because it means she can moan to an actual person about Marcie and her selfish behavior, which has gotten Mom into unnecessary trouble.

Of course I agree with everything Mom says since Marcie does get people into trouble usually all the time, even if it wasn't *this* time.

When Grandad comes home, Mom says, "If only you had been here ten minutes ago."

Grandad is very sympathetic until it is time to go watch television.

After a few minutes, he comes back and says the TV has broken down and he can't get it going.

Mom fiddles around for seven or eleven minutes while he misses his show on hedgehogs and then realizes that the batteries have gone missing. Mom says, "*That* Marcie!"

And then Marcie walks in and says,

"*What* Marcie?"

And Mom says, "I've just had Mrs. Stampney over here complaining about your soccer ball being in her birdbath and now I find you've taken the batteries out of the remote control and Grandad has had to miss the start of his wildlife hedgehog show."

Marcie says, "How could I manage to do any of that when I wasn't even here all day?"

And then Mom looks at me with very slim eyes. Because she has remembered that Marcie was at Casey's since last night.

Marcie says, "You are a lying toad, Clarice Bean."

And Mom says, "I'm inclined to agree."

I say, "But in fact Marcie is always

kicking the soccer ball over the fence and I am normally always the one being shouted at

for it so it might as well have been her."

And Mom says, "You are on very thin ice."

So I say, "And she stole my batteries from my flashlight!"

Marcie says, "Yes, but I didn't take them from the remote control, did I?"

I say, "Yes, you slightly did because if you hadn't taken my flashlight ones then I wouldn't have taken the remote controller ones, would I?"

And Mom says, "One crime does NOT cancel out another," which seems very un-right to me since the cause of my crime was utterly due to Marcie's crime. And I start to explain this, but Mom holds up her pointing finger and shakes her head and I can tell that she is in an unfair mood.

Mom says, "You need to take responsibility for your actions, Clarice Bean."

Marcie says, "Total lying toad!" and stomps upstairs.

And Mom says, "Honestly, Clarice."

Mom is in an even worser mood when Minal comes in and asks, "What's for dinner?"

She points to all the food that is now trapped in boxes and says, "NOTHING is for dinner!"

And then Marcie screeches down the stairs,

"WHO's been IN my room?

WHO's been LYING on my bed?

WHO's been READING my dog magazine?

The beagle page is all CREASED!"

She sounds a bit like that bear from the story of the three bears and so I *run* out of the house into the backyard as quickly as my flip-flops will carry me. Only they aren't *my* flip-flops.

And Marcie is right behind me.

I am trying to climb the tree but it's hard to do in these kind of shoes and one of them flips off. And Marcie grabs it and throws it over the fence, which sets Mrs. Stampney off again.

She shouts, **"DON'T IMAGINE YOU WILL BE GETTING YOUR SHOE BACK, YOUNG LADY!"**

That's when Marcie notices that she has just thrown one of her own prized possessions into Mrs. Stampney's yard.

Everything has taken a turn for the worse and I am probably going to have to stay up a tree all night and maybe longer.

It is very, very hot and I really want to come down and sit in the wading pool.

Marcie starts
throwing
fallen apples
at me.

She says some

BA

things!

Minal thinks this is very funny until I start
throwing picked-off-the-tree apples at *him*,
which makes Mom livid, and she shouts,
"Do not throw GOOD APPLES at your brother."
    And Kurt is shouting out the window for
everyone to STOP shouting because him and
Grandad are trying to watch the hedgehog show.

Everyone goes quiet.

Everyone is looking at everyone.

You can hear the breathing.

And then Marcie says in a voice
which is like a hiss,
    "And DON'T for one single minute
think YOU are ever going to have my
        rainbow skates NOW—
                    NOT for five dollars,

NOT for
nothing!"

Luckily Dad comes home with a bag of groceries and says, "I have arrived to save the day!"

Everyone is very relieved.

Until he realizes he has forgotten the two cans of tomatoes and he can't save the day without them. It turns out he has also forgotten the spaghetti.

I say, "I will *run* to Clement'ses," because, you see, I am trying to save the day and also save myself from Marcie who is spitting mad.

Clement's is the corner store and is on the corner of our street, so it doesn't take a minute to get there. It is fine to go in one flip-flop. But I have to hop because the sidewalk is as hot as toast.

Clement's is one of those good kind of stores which stocks most things that anybody would need.

I get there just when Mr. Clement is closing up. We don't know if Mr. Clement is actually named *Mr. Clement* but that's what *we* call him because he owns the shop.

I have to be really quick because he needs to cash out and get home in a hurry.

I think he wants to watch the soccer game or the tennis match or maybe he is *playing* soccer or tennis but he is definitely in a big rush.

Sometimes you go to the store to buy two cans

of tomatoes
    and some spaghetti
and nothing happens at all.

Sometimes you go to the store and they have sold out of cans of tomatoes and spaghetti, so you get the closest thing, which is a can of spaghetti in tomato sauce. It's NOT even a type of label that you have seen before—it is utterly unknown.

So you decide to get five because if there's LOTS of it maybe people will be less disappointed.

Well, this is what I do.

The other reason for buying exactly five is that the can has an OFFER for a

FREE dog identity tag and if you collect five TOKENS you can have one without paying for it. You just have to attach four first-class stamps.

We don't have an *actual* dog and so we don't *need* a dog's name tag but I like the idea of it. And maybe I could give it to Marcie because she *does* want a dog one day.

And it might make her less cross with me.

But I doubt it.

Strangely, when I come out there is an *actual*
real-life dog lurking outside the store.

He looks like he is waiting for his owner who
must be inside,

only there *was* no one inside.

He looks at me without blinking,

so I say,

"Hello,"

and give him a pat

and

walk off

home.

When I get in, it turns out that a can of spaghetti in tomato sauce is nothing like a can of tomatoes nor a package of spaghetti but it is too late to change it for something better because Mom and Dad are now in a rush. They are going to the movies, which Dad bought two tickets for and Mom forgot about and there is no other option for dinner in a hurry.

So everyone has to eat canned spaghetti on toast while they grumble.

Minal says, "What exactly in factually is it?"

I say, "Spaghetti in tomato sauce, dumdum."

Mom says, "I don't think it's THAT obvious."

Dad says, "Is it definitely for *humans*?"

Marcie says, "Why didn't you at least get spaghetti hoops?"

I say, "They only had unhooped."

Kurt says, "Why didn't you get the normal good brand in the turquoise can?"

I say, "Because they only had the green-can kind left. There was lots of it not being bought."

Dad says, "I'm NOT surprised."

I say,
"It's a new kind,
I think."

Marcie says,
"It *doesn't* taste
NEW."

Grandad says,
"It sort of tastes of **nothing**
but a little bit like
the CAN."

The problem is everyone's very hungry but no one is hungry enough to eat this. All the pantry food is in boxes and Mom says she's not prepared to unpack them until she's finished the shelves.

In the end Dad makes cheese on toast out of dryish crusts and slightly moldy old cheese from the back of the fridge.

And I am NOT popular.

It's funny how spaghetti in tomato sauce can be so delicious in a turquoise can but in a green one—unedible.

Dinner was not very pleasant and now I am slumping into a decline about the rainbow roller skates that I am never, ever going to have.

I sit there thinking, *What would **Ruby Redfort** do in this situation which is a tragedy?*

And then suddenly it pops into my head—what I need to do. I must get Marcie some more of those dog-bone flip-flops.

So I *run* to my room and empty my toadstool

bank of the three dollars and seventy-nine cents, then I ask Mom if I can *run* to the post-office-convenient store to buy Marcie a new **There's Nothing Like a … DOG** magazine.

She says, "I think that's a very wise idea."

But when I get there it turns out that they have run out completely of **There's Nothing Like a … DOG** and the new one is **There's Nothing Like a … BICYCLE**. It has a bicycle bell attached to the cover, NOT flip-flops.

It's all about bicycles and Marcie's NOT interested in those, so my putting-things-right plan is NOT going to plan.

When I come out of the post-office-convenient store, there is another dog sitting on his own outside.

Except he's the same *actual* one as the one from Clement's. I wonder who he's waiting for. I pat him on the head and *run* off home.

When I get there, Mom and Dad are on the doorstep with a suitcase.

I say, "Why are you taking a suitcase to the movies?"

Mom says, "It's a long story."

Dad says, "Grandad will explain."

Mom says, "Please don't give him anything more to worry about other than keeping an eye on you four. I am trusting you all to be responsible."

Dad says, "No floods, no fires, no fights."

Mom says, "See you on Monday."

I say, "You are going to the movies until Monday?"

Mom says, "If only we were."

Dad says, "If only we were."

Mom says, "Keep out of your sister's way until we get home!"

Dad says, "Who does that dog belong to?"

I turn around and there he is—

the same dog for the third time sitting on the sidewalk.

I think he must be following me.

Mom and Dad shout, "Be good!" and then they are off *running* to the train station.

And me and the unknown dog are left standing by the gate not knowing what to do.

I pat him on the head and then I say, "Scram," but in a nice way and it doesn't budge him.

He just sits there looking at me, not blinking.

I don't think we are speaking the same language.

I didn't get to that part in the **There's Nothing Like a ... DOG** magazine, so I am not sure how to get him to understand me.

I decide I had better take him back to Clement's corner store because his owner is probably wondering where he is.

He seems quite happy to be walking with me and he keeps looking up at me like we know each other, which I suppose we kind of do.

When I drop him back to the corner store, I give him a pat on the head and I say, "See you around." Then I walk home.

I am quite nervous when I get to our front door because I have come back without Marcie's FREE-GIFT flip-flops. I walk in very quietly, which is what **Ruby Redfort** would herself advise in these situations.

She would say, "Tread CAREFULLY so as NOT to ALERT hostile beings."

Luckily Marcie has gone upstairs to talk on the phone. I bet she is complaining about me to her friend Casey.

I discover from Grandad that the reason for Mom and Dad running to the train station with a suitcase is because Mom has not just only forgotten about the movie but also she has forgotten that they should be going to a wedding instead.

Dad forgot too so it is a double forget, which means it was almost a disaster and they could have missed their plane to who-knows-where. And if Grandad hadn't reminded them when he remembered about it, then everyone would have forgotten. Although no one can remember whose wedding Mom and Dad are going to except for Mom and Dad but they aren't here.

Grandad says, "Perhaps we should offer the movie tickets to Mrs. Stampney? Do you think that would cheer her up?" He doesn't look very excited about this idea and no one wants to knock on her door to test it out, including Grandad.

So I suggest I will pop two houses over and ask the Cushions if they would like them.

The Cushions are new to our neighborhood and we don't know their *actual* names—we just call them the Cushions because they put cushions on their doorstep and sit on them.

Everyone likes the Cushions, except for Mrs. Stampney, who is always complaining about them laughing too loudly over her fence.

Sometimes they put plants they've grown on a table outside their house with a sign that says,

IF THERE'S SOMETHING YOU LIKE, THEN PLEASE TAKE IT AND IF YOU ARE ABLE TO, THEN PUT A SMALL DONATION IN THE HONESTY BOX. ENJOY!"

Mrs. Stampney doesn't like people
selling things outside their houses,
so the Cushions are in her BAD books.

The Cushions are very pleased with the tickets
and say thank you four times each.
   One of the Cushions says,
      "What's your dog called, by the way?"
And when I turn around
      there he is again, the dog from before.
I say, "I don't know."
And they say, "You'll think of something!"
And they run off down the street in a maddish
rush because they don't want to miss the movie.
   The dog follows me back to our gate
and then plonks down. He looks hot.
   I feel bad to leave him but I don't know what
else to do. He does not understand any words,
NOT even sit or lie down.
   So how can I tell him to go home? I get some
water for him and then I wonder if I should

bring him in—just for the night.

I am about to explain to Grandad that
there is an uninvited dog by our gate
but the telephone rings and when Grandad picks
it up he looks very worried in the eyebrows.
It turns out that Peggy's neighbor's poodle, named
Violet, has slipped through the hedges and
in through Peggy's kitchen door. She is running
around her house barking at Cheeks, her cockatoo.
Peggy is terrified Violet will eat Cheeks.
Cheeks is terrified Violet will eat Cheeks. Cheeks
is now sitting on top of Peggy's ceiling light and
he won't come down.

Violet's owners are not home, so Grandad
phones up Uncle Ted to see if he can help with
the escaped poodle. Of course he goes over there
right away. Uncle Ted is good in emergencies
because he is a firefighter.
I don't think Grandad would want a
strange dog in the house in case the same
thing happened with Chirp . . .

So I decide not to ask.

I think about telling Marcie but Mom did warn
me with her pointing finger to
stay out of Marcie's way.
And when she holds up her finger it means
she is saying it STRICTLY.

Before bed I have checked on the Clement's dog
fourteen times by looking out the window.
He is still completely there looking at our door.
It's not cold outside—it's really warm, almost too
warm to sleep, and I lie in bed with just a sheet on,
utterly wide awake, wondering where this dog has
come from.

Lots of thoughts are wandering around my brain.
Maybe he is an alone dog without an owner.
Maybe somehow he heard me telling Robert
Granger that we might be getting a dog and so he
thought we might be interested in keeping him.
Maybe he didn't realize I was just making it all up.
Maybe I sort of made him appear outside
Clement's corner store. Like a wished-up dog.

If I did wish him up, then it's
my fault he is having to sleep outside
in the front yard. I think about this
and it makes me worry.

Who is responsible for him?

Maybe it's me?

When it is midnight and I can hear that everyone else isn't awake and I know that even Grandad's radio is switched off, I tiptoe downstairs.

I have to stand on the hall chair to unlock the big bolt on the front door. It's very hard to budge. And it makes a clank sound and I hold my breath.

But no one wakes up.

The dog is still there.

He is sleeping in the flower planter but as soon as I take a step he wakes up and starts wagging. So I whisper for him to follow me and we must be speaking the same language now because he understands and we tiptoe through the house and out of the back door.

I decide he can sleep in the shed at the bottom of the yard. No one ever goes in there, except for sometimes, and never Minal, because of the spiders. I run back for Mom's hand-knitted-by-Mrs.-Rogers blanket, and fill up a bowl with water and put it inside the shed, then I *creep* out and close the door.

And I hope he is not scared of spiders
because there are some
big ones
in there.

At 4:55 a.m. I am woken by a strange sound—it's quite loud but not in my room. At first I think it's the washing machine doing something strange. But then I think why would the washing machine be washing things at 4:55 a.m. when everyone is asleep?

At 5:23 I realize it must be the dog speaking his dog language, which I can't understand, so I *creep* out of bed and tiptoe down to the shed.

The sun is already up and it is quite warm.

The dog is very pleased to see me, so I lie down on the blanket and we both fall asleep.

I'm not sure what time it is when I wake up
but there is a pill bug walking up my arm. I don't
mind pill bugs and I just shake it off into a potted
plant.

The dog is still sleeping, so I carefully *creep*
out and skip up to the house. The grass is all cool
on my feet, and when I walk into the kitchen I
leave wet footprints on the floor.

I am strangely quite hungry but there is nothing
breakfast-ish to eat except for a glass of milk. And
this makes me think that maybe the Clement's dog
is hungry too.

And I wonder if dogs eat the same food as cats.
If only Betty was home—she would know the
answer.

It's still very early but even so I can hear
footsteps of everyone getting up, even Kurt who
normally sleeps late-ishly.

Grandad says it's because of the heat wave—"It's a
bit like being in a cooking pot being in this house."

At least the kitchen is still nice and cool.

Grandad is fiddling about with the kettle—he
likes to have a cup of tea the instant he wakes up.

He says, "A hot cup of tea is good
for cooling you down."

I don't understand how this can be true.

Grandad says, "I had strange dreams of wolves.
I woke up and thought I could hear one howling.
It was very realistic. I think Chirp had the
same dream because she was hopping around
in her cage."

Marcie says, "That's funny—I had *exactly* the
same dream."

Kurt says, "Pass the Puffa-Puffs."

And Minal says, "They are trapped in a box."

Of course, he is right for once.

All the breakfast and everything else that is
mainly food is trapped in a box.

So I offer to go to the corner store by myself.
You see I have a clever plan, which means I
can buy a can of dog food in SECRET with my
rainbow-skate savings from my piggy bank—

everyone will just think I am being helpful.

Unfortunately Grandad says,

"What a good idea. I'll keep you company."

And he goes to get the

wheeling-along shopping bag.

While Grandad chats to Mr. Clement, I give him the *slip*. It's a technique I learned from **Ruby Redfort**—she spends most of her time giving people the *slip*—and I quickly zip off to grab all the things we need from all the different shelves. Grandad likes chatting, so it isn't difficult for him to be distracted.

I am crouching down looking at the dog-food cans but it's hard to know which is the best type of a dog food to get because I don't know anything *about* dog food. In the end I choose the kind that is in a green can because I like the color.

Grandad only notices the can when Mr. Clement is adding everything up together but luckily he isn't wearing his good glasses, because he says, "Is that a can of that strange spaghetti we had last night?"

It does look *almost* identically the same because of the green can and the black writing.

So I say, "Yes, I might be having it for breakfast."

And Grandad says, "So long as no one's going to make me eat it."

Mr. Clement says,

"You do know it's *dog food*?"

And Grandad says,

"Yes, we had it for dinner last night."

And Mr Clement laughs, thinking we're joking about eating dog food for dinner and Grandad laughs, thinking we're talking about eating horrible spaghetti which tastes like dog food. And while they are both thinking this is funny I slip the exact money for the dog food into Grandad's pocket. This way I am not spending his money on dog food without asking.

Mr. Clement says,
"Speaking of dogs, is there any sign
of that stray puppy that was
hanging around?"

And I fidget a bit and do a shrug like I don't know.

And he says, "I was going to call the dog shelter yesterday—but then it was GONE."

Grandad says, "Is it gray? I saw a small gray dog sleeping under a bench on the hill last week."

Mr. Clement says, "Yes." And he does a big sigh and says, "It's a shame when people abandon their dogs."

I say, "How do you know it doesn't belong to someone?"

And Mr. Clement says,
"I haven't seen any posters around mentioning A MISSING DOG, and no one has asked me
to put a SIGN in my window."

Then he does another sigh and says, "And it has NO collar or tag, which means NO ONE is responsible for him." And then he itches his arm and says, "Of course it might have fleas, poor thing."

And this makes me itch my arm too.

Grandad and I wheel our shopping bag home and we unpack everything on the kitchen table.

I say, "It's such a nice day I might go and eat my breakfast in the backyard." But no one takes any notice because they are all trying to get their hands on the Puffa-Puffs.

I take the green can of dog food, a bowl, and a can opener and I sneak quickly out of the house while no one is seeing.

But when I am halfway down the yard trying to be low profile, Robert Granger suddenly pops up on the wall.

He says, "What are you doing?"

I say, "None of your business."

He says, "Is that food for your tortoise?"

I am about to tell him to buzz off when I notice Minal sitting in the sandpit—how did he get there? He is listening to EVERYTHING. I can tell by his ears.

Minal says, "We don't have a tortoise—do we?"

I say, "No."

Robert Granger says,

"Is it for your rabbit?"

I say, "No."

He says, "Because if it's for a rabbit they like cabbage— NOT food out of cans."

I say, "It ISN'T for a rabbit."

Minal says, "I don't like rabbits—they bite."

Robert Granger says,

"My rabbit doesn't bite."

I say, "Your rabbit isn't even your rabbit— it's just borrowed."

He says, "It's more than you've got."

I say, "That's what YOU think."

And then I bite my lip because I've fallen into the trap of saying TOO MUCH.

This is one of **Ruby Redfort**'s BIG DANGERS that she warns you about.

It's her agency's **RULE 1:**

KEEP IT ZIPPED.

Robert Granger says,
"OH, you have
a dog?"

Minal says,
"Do we have
a dog?"

I am wishing Robert Granger would go away or at least be more quieter—I don't want Mrs. Stampney to hear because then she will complain and the people will come and take the Clement's dog away and I will never see him again and he won't get anything to eat.

So I say, "Look, Robert Granger, we don't have a dog."

Robert Granger says, "If you don't have a dog, then why are you taking dog food into the shed?"

I say, "I'm NOT."

He says, "You are. I can see the can."

And I say, "Umm."

And Minal says, "That's not dog food—that's the horrible sgahetti from last night. I can tell by the green."

And I say, "Exactly, Robert Granger. I am having spaghetti for breakfast in the shed."

And Robert Granger says,
"So are you pretending
to have a dog?"
I say, "Why would I pretend to feed a pretend
dog pretend dog food?"
Robert Granger says,
"Because you don't have
a rabbit like me."
I say, "I can't be bothered to talk to you."
He says,
"If anyone wants to see an actual
rabbit, I've got one."
Minal says, "I do."
I say, "It's only borrowed."
Minal says, "I don't care."
And then he goes off to Robert Granger's,
which is fine with me because at least now
I can feed my
borrowed dog
in secret.

The dog seems to like the food and he eats it all and when he has finished he looks at me. I think he is wondering what we are going to do next. He's making a strange noise and I wish I had learned how to speak DOG because it sounds like what he is telling me is important.

He looks at me with a desperate face and big eyes and suddenly I know because it's the same with Minal. When my brother's face looks all desperate with big eyes, we all know what it means.

He needs to go!

I don't know that much about dogs but I do know you must scoop up afterward, so I grab one of the garden bags

and I peek out of the shed

to see if anyone is out there.

Grandad is trampling around in the flower bed trying to STOP our cat, Fuzzy, from

trampling around in the flower bed.

Everyone else is not in the kitchen,
so me and the dog make a *run* for it
through the house, out of the front door,
and on to the sidewalk.

We just make it.

It is not that nice doing the scooping part but
if you want to have a dog then you have to get
used to it. That's what I've heard my aunt saying
to my cousin Noah.

We walk up to the top of our street where the
garbage can is and I am very relieved it is so close
because no one wants to carry a bag of dog
you-know-what for much longer than a minute.
Then we *run* back home.

It is already very scorching—
TOO scorching for a dog to be in the shed.

The only thing I can do is take him upstairs
to my room. At least up here he will be far away
from Chirp and Grandad's room, which is
all the way downstairs.

I decide to carry the dog because he's not

too heavy and I don't want anyone to hear his
claws tapping on the stairs—it's just all the legs
that are difficult to manage—but
I get him the whole way
up to my bedroom
in one try.

He really likes my room. I can tell because he sniffs around and then he starts chewing Minal's anteater top.

I am just teaching him how to fetch socks without eating them when I hear my brother coming up the stairs. Luckily I am a quick thinker and manage to put the dog in the big closet. It's a walk-into one, so there's lots of room for air and breathing—I used to sit in there before I preferred the linen closet. It's full of lots of old stuff that I don't really use anymore—Mom is always saying I need to clean it out.

The dog starts right away chewing an enormous-ish white cardigan, which is dangling off a shelf, and I quietly close the door.

When Minal comes in, I am pretending to sit on my bed when I in actual fact am trying to think of a distraction to get him to go away. But then the phone rings and nobody is answering it, so *I* have to *run* down to get it. I always like to answer the phone because you never know who it might be and it could be important or even an emergency.

It turns out to be just Mom and Dad calling to say they have safely arrived in wherever they have gone, and to say hello to everyone but they can't talk now because they are late for wherever they are meant to be next and will call later when they have more time. I put down the phone and then at that exact second I hear

a very LOUD squealing sound.
When I *run* into my room,
my brother is *running* out.

It is hard to hear what he is saying because of the shrieking but it's something like,

"There's a ghost
in the closet!
There's a ghost
in the
closet!"

I am wondering why he thinks it is a ghost when it is an *actual* alive dog but when I open the closet door I can see what he means because the white cardigan has fallen on top of the dog and so it does look a bit like a moving-around ghost.

Although it has red buttons down the middle and ghosts do not.

While Minal is running downstairs to tell Grandad about the closet ghost, I decide to move the dog into the bathroom. The problem is when I try the door Marcie is in there and she shouts, "I'm taking a bath!" Then she shouts, "If that's you, Clarice Bean, then

keep away from my roller skates and keep away from me."

She has NOT come off the boil and I don't think she ever will.

Even with *her* shouting I can STILL hear Minal who is squarking at Grandad. He sounds a bit like Chirp but less in tune.

He is saying, "You have to get it out of the closet."

And Grandad says, "Righto, I'll just get a glass and a piece of paper."

And Minal is saying, "It's much bigger than that."

And Grandad says, "Don't worry—this is a very large glass. Then we'll just put him out the window."

Minal is saying, "You can't put ghosts out the window. They just come back."

And Grandad says, "Oh, I thought you were talking about a spider."

I am panicking slightly because I need to quickly hide the dog before Grandad comes up the stairs. I decide the best place to hide out is in Marcie's room since she will be in the bath forever. She always is.

We slip in and close the door and I say to the dog, "You need to keep it zipped." And he seems to understand.

By the time Grandad comes upstairs to prove to Minal that there is not a ghost in the closet, there is just a cardigan on the floor.

While I am waiting for them to go downstairs again and for the coast to be clear, the dog starts to get bored. It is hard to keep him quiet, so I have to let him chew Marcie's makeup bag. While I am watching him, I am wondering what kind of name would suit him and would it be something to do with chewing?

I can hear Grandad using his sensible voice. He only has one voice and it's *always* sensible.

Luckily he is good at calming people down and he says, "Let's go out in the backyard. I'll fill up the wading pool and you can dip your feet in it—it will take your mind off the ghost. You know they DON'T like water?"

Minal says, "What if it's a mermaid ghost?"

And Grandad says, "Well, if it *was* a mermaid ghost, then how did it manage to get upstairs into the closet?

Mermaids DON'T have legs, you know."

I am listening at the door, waiting for a chance to sneak back into my room, when I hear Marcie padding along in her bare feet.

Instantly me and the dog quickly scrabble under her bed. He doesn't seem to mind at all. He looks happy to be hiding out.

Marcie walks in and I can see her feet stopped almost exactly in front of where we are lying. She picks up her makeup bag and then right away drops it.

And out loud she says,

"Clarice Bean, you *creep*, what have you done to my makeup bag? Why is it all chewed?"

I think it is very unfair that she right away thinks it is *my* fault. It could easily not be me. I am *frozen* with fear and too panicked to move, which is lucky because I mustn't make a twitch. It's something ***Ruby Redfort*** says:

PANIC CAN FREEZE YOUR BRAIN,

which is what has happened to me.

But unfortunately the dog is NOT *frozen*
in the brain with PANIC at all and he licks
Marcie on the foot, which makes her scream.
Until she sees his nose poking out,
and she says in

a very quiet voice,

"There is a dog under my bed."

Which is the kind of thing
that doesn't need saying
because it's obvious.

I decide I might as well slither out because
I can't hide under here forever and also I've got
pins and needles in my left or right leg—I can't
even tell which one it is anymore because
it is utterly numb to the bone.

Marcie has got her mouth open in that way
people do when they are just about to shout
something slightly rudely or surprisedly
but nothing comes out.

Like in the cartoons.

She looks at me with her eyes gone big.
Then she says, "Where did it come from?"

And I say, "I think I might have wished him up."

And she says, "What do you mean?"

So I say,

"He just appeared and then he sort of
started following me. It wasn't my idea—

he came up with it on his own."

She says, "You are saying

he followed you into my *bedroom*?"

I say, "No, he followed me *home* and then

we were hiding out because I was worrying
Minal would tell—he's such a little big mouth.
And I don't want him to say anything to *Grandad*
because he will worry that Chirp
might be eaten."

She says, "But WHO does the dog *belong* to?"

I say, "He doesn't belong to anyone."

She says, "How do you know?"

I say, "Mr. Clement was talking about him
to Grandad and they both were saying
how he's a stray who was on the hill
living under the bench and Mr. Clement was
going to call the dog-collector people
because no one is responsible for him.
This dog is a dog on his own."

Marcie looks like she might cry.

Marcie never cries except if it is to do with
dogs being sad.

I say, "I don't think he wants to go to the
dog-rescue place because otherwise he
wouldn't have followed me."

Marcie nods and says,
"I think we should
keep him."

I say,

"I do too."

She says, "At least for now."

And I say,

"And maybe longer."

She says, "I mean he *has* chosen *our* house
and if he likes it here he should live here . . .
probably."

I am remembering what Mr. Clement said
about the collar and the name tag.
And I say, "If we name him,
        then he's ours and NOT a stray.
    I mean, if we get a collar and a name tag
for him, then he won't be lost anymore.
        WE will be
            responsible for him."

Marcie makes a face, which means she is
thinking. Then she says, "That's *true*."

I say,
    "In fact, I have a tag for him.
It's not sent off for yet but it's a FREE OFFER
        from the horrible-spaghetti people—
    we could send it today.
And if you include two first-class stamps
        plus two more then you can get his
                    name scratched on it."

Marcie says, "But what *is* his name?"

I say, "Well, I have had a few ideas . . .

One is Spaghetti."

I look at Marcie and she shakes her head.
She says,

"You have to think how it will be
calling Spaghetti across the park."

I think about this and I decide I don't want to
SHOUT "Spaghetti" across the park, especially
if anyone I know is around, or that boy Karl,
who is in my class.

I don't even like spaghetti. Only sometimes.
I like it the way Dad does it with the tomato-ish
sauce he makes and I like it with cheese and
sometimes Bolognese but otherwise not really
so much, unless Peggy or Granny makes it,
then I like it with anything.

Marcie says, "So what's your other name idea?"

I say, "My other name idea is Tomato."

Marcie says,

"Where are you getting these ideas from?"

I say, "It's what I was shopping for when I first met him."

She says, "*Where* were you shopping? The post office? Because you can't call him Postoffice."

I say, "No, it was the corner store. You know, Clement's. That's where I found him. He was lurking about outside on his own, waiting for someone who wasn't there but we can't call him Cornerstore either."

Marcie ignores this and says,

"So you *first* saw him outside *Clement's*?"

And I say, "Yes."

Then we both look at each other in the eyes at the exact same moment.

And we both say,

"Clement!"

Except actually I say *Clement's* but Marcie
says it's better without the *S*.

And our dog starts
        wagging his tail
  like we have
      guessed his name
        finally.

Marcie quickly fills in the spaghetti form with our name and address, and I fill in the little squares to tell them what dog name we would like written on the tag. You have to put it carefully in CAPITALS exactly in the little squares on the form and you can't mess up.

Then I pop the five tokens in the envelope and Marcie searches around on Mom's desk for four stamps. They add up to about two-and-a-half-ish dollars if you had to buy them, so I take $1.20 from my toadstool and Marcie does the same and we put it in Mom's drawer so it's not actually taking the stamps without paying.

We have to check for the coast to be clear before we can get down the stairs and out of the front door.

Marcie says, "No one must see us with Clement."

And I say, "Especially not Minal."

And she says,

"He can't keep a SECRET without telling."

Which is exactly what everyone knows.

Marcie says, "Maybe wear something long so we can tuck Clement under it."

I say, "Won't I look a bit suspicious?"

She says, "You can just pretend you are dressing up. No one will think that's strange."

The only long trailing thing I can find is Mom's kimono, which I am a bit nervous of borrowing because it is strictly NOT allowed.

As soon as we get out into the street, we see the Cushions walking towards us. But we can't get Clement to hide under the kimono—he is too excited about being outside.

He just stands there, wagging his tail.

And the Cushions stop to pet him and they say,
"Hello, dog. Do you have a name yet?"
And me and Marcie say,
"Clement," both at the same time.
And one of the Cushions says, "Like the store?"
And we say, "Yep, the same as that."
And the other Cushion says,
"Hello, Clement. Where are you off to?"
And Marcie says,
"We are just taking him for a walk."
And the Cushions say, "What a good idea to
wear a kimono. It will keep the sun off you."
And I say, "That's what I thought."
Which is slightly not true but sometimes
it's good to agree when you are trying to act
unstrangely. We decide it doesn't matter if the
Cushions know we now have a dog because they
are new to the neighborhood and they will think
it is completely normal.
We go all the way up
Navarino Street . . .

and on to the hill and then Clement runs arou

just runs in circle

...out he doesn't run away.

It turns out Marcie knows quite a LOT about dogs. She knows that when they are young they aren't meant to go on very long walks. It is bad for their legs or something. We don't actually know *how old* Clement is but you can tell he is not a fully finished dog yet.

He is obviously learning our language because when we say it's time to go he comes with us right away. On the way down, we can feel the breeze blowing into our faces but by the time we get to the bottom it has disappeared.

We reach the gate, and Marcie stops to tie her shoelace and then she looks up and says,

"You can *have* my rainbow roller skates if you still want them."

And it's hard to speak because of course

I am AMAZED.

I say, "How come you have changed your mind?"

And she says,

"Because you found a dog."

I know what she means.

Because I know my sister has *always* wanted a dog, so she doesn't care anymore about the FREE-GIFT flip-flops or the creased beagle in a beret. All she cares about is having a real *actual* dog.

I say, "But the problem is I have spent all my savings on dog food and stamps and so I haven't even got the three dollars now—

I've only got the seventy-nine cents."

And she says, "It's OK. You can just have them."

I say, "Thanks, Marcie."

And she says, "You're welcome."

And then we keep walking to the post office.

We don't go straight home after we mail the form. Instead we stop off to buy some more dog food with the rest of Marcie's pocket money.

Then we go into **Furry-Fins Pet Shop** and we ask the lady—who is named Jackie, written on a name tag—which sort of food we should buy, and she says, "How old is your dog?"

And we say, "He's a rescued one,
so it's hard to be sure."

And she says, "Well, I can see he's still
a puppy, so I would recommend . . ."
and then she looks at the shelves and
picks up a can. "This one!"

The problem is we can only afford *one* can
and a small bag of the dried-up food.

And we need to buy a leash and a collar
and all the other thingummyjigs.

Marcie writes down all the things on a piece
of paper and next to them all the prices.

We tell Jackie that we will come back soon
when we have the shopping bag with wheels
so it will be easier to carry everything.

We don't want her to know that we don't
have the money or she will wonder why
Mom and Dad aren't helping.
Marcie says,

"We have to seem like
responsible people."

The dog leash I really want most has rainbow stripes and it will look good with my NEW rainbow roller skates but Marcie says we might not be able to afford such an expensive leash.

She says, "We have to be practical."

She says, "First of all we need to think how we can find the money to get all the things we absolutely need and have to have."

And that's when I think of a really good idea. I say, "We can sell stuff."

And Marcie says, "What stuff?"

And I say, "All the stuff in my walk into closet, which is getting in the way, and also that stuff Mom has left out for donating."

Marcie says, "What stuff?"

I say, "In the box in the corner of the laundry room."

And Marcie says, "But where are we going to sell it?"

And I say, "Outside our house, like the

Cushions do sometimes when they sell their homemade plants—we can set up the wobbly table on the sidewalk and sell all the stuff we don't want anymore."

And this is what we do.

It takes a long time to carry everything out and the clothes box is overflowing and I am not sure what is for donation and what is meant for ironing, so in the end I have to sort of guess.

We set it all up in a way that makes it look like it's worth buying. Marcie says it's important to display everything well because then people can see that it might be nicer than they thought.

She is right about this because once we have covered the table in Mom's NEW Christmas tablecloth and put everything out I am wondering why we don't want to keep it.

Marcie makes a sign which says,

"Antiques for sale" and another one

which says, "Everything for sale
except the tablecloth and the kimono!"

I write the prices on some stickers with a
PINK marker pen and then we stick them
on everything. Marcie says it makes it easier
for people to make up their minds if they know
the prices.

Marcie is wearing a sun hat with a sticker with
50 cents written on it, a jacket that has $1.50
clipped to it, and a skirt over her shorts which says
25 cents. She is wearing the shorts underneath just
in case anyone wants to buy the skirt.

She says, "This way people can see how it all
looks." She seems to know a LOT about selling
things. It's quite hot sitting there on chairs in the
sun although there is a biggish tree in front of
our house.

The shade keeps moving so in the end we go
and fetch the striped umbrella.

It helps keep the sun off our faces but even so
Marcie is finding she is sticking to her chair.

There is **utterly**
NOT a *whisk* of a
b r e e z e.

EVERYTHING
FOR SALE
EXCEPT THE TABLECLOTH
AND THE KIMONO!

7

I am wearing my NEW roller skates. I'm not
actually rollering in them—I'm just sitting on
a chair behind our table—but I like the feel of
them even if they aren't going anywhere.

Clement falls asleep under the table while we
wait and wait for the shoppers.

After ten minutes we are beginning to worry that
maybe no one will come. But then all of a sudden
we have several customers and we manage
to sell my Teeny Pocket Pet collection,
five pairs of tights which have gone TOO tight,
my How to Make Pictures Out of String Kit,
and a puzzle of some bears drinking out of
teacups, plus quite a lot of old junk Mom was
getting rid of, like saucers that don't have cups
anymore due to breakages.

Mrs. Papadopoulos says she can use them to
stand her potted plants on.

Also we sell a pair of oldish curtains that are
slightly frayed at the bottom—our neighbor Elena

says she can shorten them, so that's not a problem. Marcie sells her rubber-band-bracelet-maker thing and a dream catcher I would like to buy myself but Marcie says we must not buy anything off our own stall or there is no point selling it. Two people at once want to buy Kurt's orange T-shirt, which is not surprising because it's almost new. I don't know why he put it with the donations.

Absolutely no one wants Minal's caterpillar slippers.

By two o'clock we are beginning to get peckish and everyone has *vanished* except for a couple of bumblebees.

Marcie says all the people have gone to the hill to sunbathe.

They like to go there on hot days and lie flat out on the grass.

Marcie counts up all of the change we have collected. She says, "It still isn't quite enough. We are exactly five dollars short."

Which makes us a bit down in the dumps.

We are about to decide to fold up and take the things inside but then we notice a tall girl in blue shorts walking toward us.

Marcie says, "Let's wait for this one person just in case she is a customer."

When she gets to our table she peers at everything carefully and picks up a snow globe with an Eiffel Tower in it and I hold my breath. You see I slightly don't really want to sell that. Then she puts it down and I am relieved and also disappointed because we *need* her to buy it.

I say, "Is there anything particular you are looking for?" Because they often say this in the stores. And the girl points at Marcie's sweatshirt, which is hanging on a hanger by the doorstep, and she says, "How much for that?"

So I say, "One or two dollars I think."

And Marcie says, "One dollar and fifty cents."

And the girl asks if she can take a look at it, so I stand up and skate over to the front door to get it.

Then the girl in the blue shorts says,

"Hey, I like your skates,"

and she looks at the notice that says,

EVERYTHING FOR SALE

EXCEPT THE TABLECLOTH AND THE KIMONO!

And she says, "Are they for sale?"

And I look at Marcie and she looks at me

and I say, "Umm . . ."

And the girl says, "They are super cool."

And I say, "I know."

And it's hard to say YES because I have *always*

wanted these roller skates ever since Marcie first

got them and now they are *actually* mine.

And I look at Marcie and I think about how

she really wants this dog, and how dogs need

LOTS of things.

And if we are going to be responsible for him

then we must get him a collar and a leash to

prove he is ours.

So I say, "They are five dollars."

The girl says, "DONE!"

And I bite my lip a bit too hard and it slightly
begins to puff up.

Marcie whispers, "But you love those skates."

But all my words have dried up and I can't even
say, "I know."

And I quite slowly pull at the bow of my loopy
laces and I feel sad that I haven't even been to
the end of Navarino Street in them.

Marcie says, "Are you *sure*?"

And I just nod.

I hand them to the girl in the blue shorts and
when she puts them on I am secretly hoping
they won't fit.

But they do.

She says,

"I love them. I really love them."

And I say, "So do I."

And she says,

"But then why are you

selling them?"

And Marcie says, "Because she is trying to help someone else."

And then we explain about our lost dog and how we want to keep him.

Marcie says, "You see, we need the money to buy him a collar and stuff."

I say, "Dogs have to have collars or people won't know they belong to someone."

The girl agrees. She says, "That's true."

She smiles at me. "Well, it is really nice of you." Then she reaches in her purse and hands us two more dollars.

"Here, for your dog—thanks for
    selling your roller skates.
        I promise to look after them."

And then she skates away.

Marcie gives me a touch on the arm and says,
"You can always ask for rainbow roller skates
on your Christmas list." And I know she is trying
to cheer me up.

But I say, "I don't think there are any more
rainbow roller skates—rainbow ones are very
unusual."

We are so hot and all we can hear is wasps
and bees buzzing. Everyone else is lying down.

We pack up all the unsold odds and ends and
drag it all back inside.

When we fold up the tablecloth, we notice the
marker pen I was using to write the prices on

the stickers has leaked out and there is a big blot in the shape of a heart.

Marcie says, "I don't think that's ever going to wash out."

We have to stop for a quick snack and a glass of water and then we go off to **Furry-Fins**.

This time we take the shopping bag on wheels with us.

We get everything on our list and due to the extra $2 from the blue-shorts girl, we can even afford the rainbow leash.

There is just enough left over for a Yogga-Pop. One each.

As we are coming around the corner into Navarino Street, we see Kurt walking down the road toward the house.

Marcie whispers, "*Quick!* Put Clement under the kimono—we'll pretend we're chatting until he goes inside."

But Kurt doesn't go inside. He walks past the

house and right toward where we are standing.

Marcie whispers, "Act casual."

So I try to think what **Ruby Redfort** would do. She would probably blow a bubble-gum bubble but I don't have any bubble gum. Dad banned it when some got stuck to the sofa cushion, which he sat on, and it transferred to his second-best pants.

He was quite upset.

And now bubble gum is not allowed.

Kurt says, "How come you are hanging out here?"

I can't talk because my Yogga-Pop is all stuck in my teeth.

Marcie says, "Why? Is it against the law or something?"

And he says, "I was just asking."

Marcie says, "We've just been selling some stuff—that's all."

And I manage to say, "Outside the house like the Cushions do."

Kurt says, "What stuff?"

And Marcie says, "That box of old donations in the laundry room."

Kurt says, "My T-shirt was lying on top of that box—I hope you didn't sell that?"

Marcie looks at me and I say, "Mainly we just sold old stuff from my bedroom."

And then Kurt says, "Did you use the money to buy THAT dog?"

And I say, "What dog?"

And he says, "The one under Mom's kimono. Are you unaware of it?"

And I say, "Oh, I wonder where that came from?"

And Kurt says, "You have it on a leash!"

And Marcie says, "Promise you won't tell?"

And Kurt says, "It's not me telling that you need to worry about—Mom's going to find out anyway as soon as she sees THAT."

And then we both see what he means because Clement has chewed a big hole in the bottom of Mom's kimono.

And then we tell Kurt the whole story.

He says, "You know you can't keep it
a SECRET forever?"

And we say, "Just until Mom and Dad get back."

And I say, "We are trying to prove that we are
very responsible and then maybe we would
be allowed to keep him."

Kurt pats him on the head and says,
"He's a really nice dog. What's his name?"

And we say, "Clement."

Kurt says, "Like the store?"

And I say, "Yep, like the store."

And he says, "Don't worry. I won't tell.
But don't let Grandad see him or he will worry
about Chirp."

And Marcie says,
"And DON'T tell Minal!"

And I say, "Because he is a LITTLE big mouth!"

And Marcie says, "I'm really sorry
but I think we *did* sell your T-shirt."

But, strangely, Kurt isn't even upset.

Now that there are three of us who know about the secret dog there are fewer people to find out about him, so we don't have to worry so much.

We come up with a sort of plan.

Kurt says he can take Clement once around the block just before bed because dogs always need to go once around the block just before bed.

He says, "But what are we going to do with him for now?"

I say, "I have been hiding him in the shed. Minal never goes in there. He's too scared of the spiders."

Marcie says, "Won't it be too hot?"

I say, "I've opened the two windows and it's coolened down a lot because the big tree gives it the after-lunch shade."

Marcie goes in to test it out and when she's sure it's fine for a human being, she decides it will be fine for a dog being too. Then we get on with our plan.

Kurt says, "I will distract Minal and you can make a *run* for it."

It's easy to distract Minal when you want to.

All you have to do

is tickle him.

Marcie distracts Grandad by telling him a very complicated thing that happened once at school, and Grandad is finding it hard to keep up.

He keeps saying, "Who did you say fell into the swimming pool?"

Neither of them notice me and Clement slipping out of the back door.

While I am fluffing up Clement's blanket, and giving him his food, I can hear the telephone ringing.

Minal shouts,

"Clarice Bean, Mom and Dad are on the telephone from another country and you have to come right now!"

Of course Robert Granger straight away pops up on the wall. He *always* wants to know what other people are up to because it's *always* more interesting than what he is up to.

Robert says,
"Why are your mom and dad
in another country?
Why are they on
the telephone?
Why were you in the shed?
Are you feeding your
pretend dog?"

I leave him to bother Minal with his
        none-of-his-business questions,
                and I *run* inside.

It is interesting to hear Mom and Dad's news.
They say the married couple are floating around
in a hot-air balloon but will be down in time
for dinner.

To me it seems quite exciting but they both
sound very bored about it.

Dad says, "I'm SO hungry I could eat a can of
horrible spaghetti."

Mom says, "I am SO hungry I could eat *Dad*."

By the time we have finished chatting, it is time
for our *own* supper.

Grandad decides it is too hot to cook and so he
sends Kurt and Marcie out to fetch fish and chips
from the fish-and-chip place.

Everybody is happy about this
        because everybody likes fish and chips.

Before I sit down to eat my food, I pop out to
check on Clement.

He seems very happy. He is busy chewing a dog toy in the shape of an elephant and he doesn't even look up when I go to leave.

The fish and chips have made everyone in an extra good mood at the table and it is all pleasant except for Minal, who is talking with his mouth full as usual. He is burbling on about nothing and talking about Robert Granger next door and no one is interested until he says,

"I think there's a dog living in our shed."

Marcie splurts water all over the table.

But Kurt just keeps eating chips like no one has said anything important, so I do the same.

It's a **Ruby Redfort** tactic.

RULE 22:

IF YOU THINK YOU MIGHT TALK YOURSELF INTO A TRAP, KEEP YOUR TRAP SHUT.

Grandad says, "This morning you said there was a ghost in the closet."

Minal says, "There is a ghost in the closet. I saw it."

Grandad says, "*And* a dog in the shed?"

Minal says, "Yes, Robert says Clarice is feeding it sgahetti in a can."

I say, "Robert Granger is *always* making things up that aren't even true."

Minal says,

"But Robert says he heard

barking coming out of the shed?"

Kurt says, "It was probably Clarice. She is trying to make Robert *envious* by *pretending* we have a dog."

Marcie says, "Yes, Clarice is just pretending to have a dog. It's just a pretend one."

Grandad says,

"PRETEND dogs
are the BEST kind.

I'm sure Peggy wishes Violet was a pretend dog. Imagine if she had swallowed poor Cheeks."

Marcie looks at me and I look at Kurt and Kurt makes a face. Clement must not see Chirp or something bad might happen.

Grandad doesn't take any notice of Minal. He says, "Now, why don't we all sit down and watch television together?"

Everybody likes this idea especially because the living room is less sweltering than all the other rooms.

Watching TV makes us forget our worries,
and even Minal has instantly forgotten
about the possible dog in the shed.

But it doesn't last.

A howling sound comes in through the kitchen window and drifts all the way into the living room and Marcie has to turn the TV up really loudly so Grandad won't wonder who it is. Luckily Minal thinks it's coming from upstairs.

He says, "I think I can hear the ghost again. He's definitely still in the closet."

Grandad says, "Do you think maybe it's time for bed?"

But Minal says he won't step one toe in our room. He says he knows the ghost will get out of the closet and sit on him in the night.

He says, "I am not sleeping with a ghost."

While Grandad is busy trying to calm Minal down, Kurt manages to *sneak* Clement out through the house because Marcie is sure he might need

a you-know-what

but in fact it slightly turns out to be TOO LATE
as he has already peed on Mom's hand-knitted-
by-Mrs.-Rogers blanket.

Marcie says, "Well, at least it was only pee."

But I'm not sure Mom will think that since
now *three* actual things of hers have been ruined,
including a kimono and a Christmas tablecloth.

By the time Kurt and Clement get back from
their walk around the block, the problem of
where to put Clement has been solved.

Minal says he wants to sleep with Grandad, so
Grandad has to have him in *his* room in a
sleeping bag even though it's much too hot
for sleeping bags. He looks like a

biggish maggot
lying on
the carpet.

Grandad says, "Let's all just go to bed.
We'll deal with that ghost in the morning.
It's too late to think about it now."
So Clement sleeps in my room
and no one has to sleep in the shed.
He seems to like it under the bed with
Marcie on the floor next to him.

And everyone is relieved
because no one wants
to sleep with the

spiders.

A fly wakes me up really early. It is circling around my room very slowly because it is **too hot** to **buzz** around quickly.

It wakes Marcie up too. She shakes my arm and says, "We need to take Clement for his *you-know-what.*"

I scramble myself out of the tangled-up sheet and look for my left slipper, which has crept under my bed and is slightly wet from being chewed. But in fact it is **too hot** for slippers.

I look at myself in the bathroom mirror—my hair is all st**u**ck to my face with heat and I look a bit **hot** in the cheeks.

We decide to go out in our nighties because they are very cool and they could be summer dresses if you decided they were. Clement licks my knees and we go downstairs. Very, very quietly.

Marcie and I look for Clement's rainbow leash but the funny thing is we just can't find it.

It's completely gone.

We search everywhere.

Kurt says, "I think it got accidentally dropped in the yard."

He says, "Clement was chewing it and I was trying to get him inside before Grandad saw us. I had to throw his elephant to get him to let go."

So I *run* out to look but there is no sign of the elephant or the leash. I even crawl into the flower bed and I am just beginning to think the leash has utterly vanished when I see Minal walk into the backyard.

He has the elephant attached
to Clement's rainbow leash and he is
dragging it around, pretending it is a pet.
Before I can march up and grab it,
Mrs. Stampney pops her head over the fence
and says, "Was that your dog barking at
my cat yesterday evening?"
  And Minal says,
    "No, we don't have a real dog.
Clarice has a pretend one in the shed
    but we have an *actual* ghost in
  the closet upstairs."
Mrs. Stampney says,
    "WHAT on EARTH are you
        BABBLING about?"

Minal says, "The ghost in the cupboard.
Did you hear it howling?"

Mrs. Stampney says, "I'm NOT interested in
howling ghosts. I'm interested in barking dogs."

Minal says, "Robert says our pretend dog barks
but it doesn't. It eats sgahetti out of a can."

Mrs. Stampney says, "Oh for goodness' sake!"

Then she disappears and Minal goes off to sit in
his sand pit with the elephant.

And I grab the rainbow leash and Marcie,
Clement, and I race out of the house as quickly as
we can.

The sidewalk isn't too heated up to walk on
but we decide to skip just in case.

We don't bump into anyone we know except
for the Cushions. They are putting out their little
table with their homemade plants but no one else
is around.

It is fun having a dog to walk,
and we all *run*

around and around and around.

Only the dog people are out.

Grandad wants to make sure everything upstairs is shipshape by the time Mom and Dad get home. So I have to explain to Clement that he needs to stay in the downstairs bathroom while I wait for Grandad to check our rooms for tidiness.

Clement doesn't seem to mind so I leave him there and *run* upstairs.

Minal is standing outside our bedroom door, talking through the gap. He is trying to explain to Grandad where his clean clothes are without stepping a toe inside. He won't go in because of the ghost.

I secretly hope he might decide to move into Grandad's room for always. I would rather share with a ghost than a younger brother.

Grandad is looking for Minal's green top, which is difficult because ALL his clothes are on the floor and the floor is mainly green.

Minal says he only wants to wear this one with the anteater on it but when Grandad finds it, it turns out to have been strangely chewed, and this sets Minal off again.

He is whimpering, "It's eaten my anteater top."

Grandad says, "No, no, ghosts don't have teeth." But he doesn't sound as sure about it as he did before.

He looks relieved when the doorbell pings and we can all go downstairs.

It's Sandra from nice-next-door.

She says, "I'm so sorry to ask but would you mind helping me fix the electric fan? I am absolutely sweltering."

Grandad is good at fixing things, so people are always asking him stuff like this.

No one minds because Sandra is not Mrs. Stampney and if you kick a soccer ball into her yard she will give it straight back.

Grandad calls out, "Tell Kurt he is in charge and if there is an emergency, just squeal. I'll only be over the fence."

As soon as the front door closes, there is a very loud screech and when I turn around I see Minal toppling backward, being licked in the face by the dog, who has escaped from the downstairs bathroom.

Minal is very flustered and quite shocked.

He says, "The pretend dog just licked me in the face."

Just exactly then, Marcie calls out, "Mom and Dad are coming down the road. I can see them from the window!"

Kurt says, *"Quick!* Hide Clement!"

I say, "Minal, you are not to tell!"

Minal says, "I won't."

I say, "You better promise!"

And he says, "I promise."

And we put Clement back where he was and try to act natural.

We open the front door and there are Mom and Dad. They look very happy to be home, though a bit hot in the cheeks. And we ask them lots of questions about their trip.

Mom says, "I am desperate for a cup of

tea and a sit-down, but if I don't change into something cool, I think I'll melt. How did it get to be so hot?"

Dad says, "It's so humid it could rain."

Mom says, "Yes, it feels like thunder."

Dad says, "I'll take a dip and then come back down."

Kurt carries their suitcase up to their room, Marcie runs Dad a bath, and I fetch them some cool drinks. Mom says, "Goodness, you are *all* being so helpful!"

Dad says, "Why are you all being so helpful?"

Mom says, "Yes, why are you all being so helpful?"

I say, "It's just nice to have you back."

Then I run down to check on Clement but strangely he is no longer in the downstairs bathroom. I run around trying to find where he has gone, then I catch sight of him through the kitchen window.

He is sitting in the wading pool with Minal. He has the rainbow leash clipped to his collar.

I rush into the garden but just as I get there Robert Granger pops onto the wall, and he is holding the rabbit.

He says, "Hey, you do have a dog!"

I say, "Can you talk any louder?"

He says, "What's his name? Do you think he likes rabbits?"

And then he climbs down
into our actual yard
and Clement looks up,
and the rabbit wriggles,
and Robert
lets go …

and the rabbit *runs*
and Clement squeaks and
jumps out of the wading pool …

and *runs*
toward
the fence.

He disappears
through the hole
and into
Mrs. Stampney's
yard.

There is a

scream.

Then a LOUD rumbling noise
and a cracking sound,
and suddenly it is
pouring
with
rain.

And the next thing we know the doorbell is PINGING nonstop.

Mom rushes downstairs and when she opens the door Mrs. Stampney is on the step with a purple face.

Mrs. Stampney is not put off by lightning or thunder. She shouts,

"Are you actually aware that there is a dog right now in my yard walking on my new patio which my brother-in-law
has just concreted down?"

Mom says,
"Well, for once, Mrs. Stampney,
I am very certain that this has nothing to do with us so please shout your complaints at someone who *actually* has a dog!"

Mrs. Stampney shouts,
"I am shouting my complaints at you because it's your dog!"

Mom shouts,

"Mrs. Stampney, either you have lost your mind or I have lost my mind because I'd like to know how I managed to acquire a dog when I have been at a very boring wedding all weekend."

Mrs. Stampney says,

"I SAW him with my own two eyes STANDING on MY patio!"

By now Dad has gotten out of the bath and dripped downstairs. He has missed what the shouting is all about and says,

"What's the problem with someone standing on a patio? Isn't that what patios are for?"

Mrs. Stampney goes even more purpler.
She shouts,
"THE CEMENT WASN'T SET!
NOW I AM GOING TO
HAVE TO LIVE FOR THE
REST OF MY DAYS WITH
DOG PRINTS IN MY PATIO
AND I HATE
DOGS!"

Mom shouts,

"Well, I'm sorry to hear that,
Mrs. Stampney, but I suggest you
GO and find the owner of
this dog and
SHOUT
at THEM!"

And that's when Grandad walks up the path.
He is soaked to the bone, and next to him,
attached to the rainbow leash,
is Clement.

He says,
"Good morning, Mrs. Stampney.
I have just found our dog.
I do hope he didn't give you
any trouble?
I think he got into your yard through
a HOLE in your fence.
You might want to
get it fixed."

And Mom looks at Clement,

and Grandad looks at Mom,

and we all hold our breath.

And Mom says,

"Oh, of course, that *is* our dog."

And for once Mrs. Stampney is speechless
and has utterly nothing
to say back.

I am very excited
            when I find
the envelope on the doormat
                    addressed to me.

I know it's from the horrible-spaghetti people
because it's in a green envelope and has a
picture of the spaghetti can on the sticky label.
When I shake it, the metal tag falls out and I see
our last name is on the back with our telephone
number. It looks good.

I turn it over and I read the name.

It's scratched neatly on there.

        It says CLEMENT except
                    there is no L.

And Marcie looks at it and says,
   "*Maybe* you missed it.

               Do you think you did?"
And I think I was concentrating too hard on
fitting the letters inside the boxes to remember
the *L*, and I say,
            "I probably did."
Marcie says, "I like it."
Dad says, "It's the perfect name for a dog who
has just left his paw prints cemented in
Mrs. Stampney's patio."
   But I'm not sure Clement will like it.
It's not his name.
   Marcie says we should ask Grandad because he
knows about animals.

Grandad is talking to Chirp,
               and Chirp is singing
                              a
                               tune.

She is perched on Clement-with-no-*L*'s head and
Fuzzy is playing with his tail. He doesn't even mind.

Marcie says, "Grandad, how did you know
that this dog would be a bird-friendly,
cat-friendly dog?"

And he says, "I think when I saw him running
away from Robert's rabbit."

I say, "You mean the borrowed rabbit."

And Grandad says, "Yes, that borrowed rabbit
really gave him the frights and, as we all know,
Mrs. Stampney's yard is not a sensible place
to hide if you're scared of scary things."

I say, "Yes, it's lucky you were there."

And Marcie says, "But HOW were you *there*
when you were supposed to be over at nice
Sandra's house?"

And Grandad says, "Because I heard a commotion."

And I say, "But I thought your ears were on the
outs?"

And Grandad says, "It was a very loud
commotion, so I took a peek over the fence

and thought your dog might need some help."

And Marcie says, "How did you know we even had a dog?"

And he says, "Because I was beginning to wonder how a ghost had managed to chew a hole in Minal's anteater T-shirt. Ghosts don't have teeth, you know."

I say, "He has ruined lots of Mom's things too. She might not want him when she finds out."

And Grandad says, "This dog seems to be the one thing everybody in this family does agree on. Even your mother wants Clement to stay."

And then I tell Grandad about the gone-wrong tag with the missing *L*.

I say, "Do you think Clement will like his name now it has a lost letter?"

And Grandad says,

    "Why don't you try calling him?"
So we do,
and straight away he looks up and licks Marcie on the knee and I can tell he is definitely smiling.

And that's how we know Cement must be his
        actual name because he knows
    it belongs to him
            and that he belongs
                    to us.

More exceptionOrdinarily good books
by Lauren Child

THE CLARICE BEAN NOVELS:

★ Clarice Bean, ★ IN
GLORIOUS
COLOR
★ Think Like An Elf ★ ★*

Utterly Me,
Clarice Bean

Clarice Bean
Spells Trouble

Clarice Bean,
Don't Look Now

THE CLARICE BEAN PICTURE BOOKS:

Clarice Bean,
That's Me

Clarice Bean,
Guess Who's Babysitting?

I would like to thank the following for all their talent, support, and inspiration:

Goldy Broad, Sam Stewart, Nick Lake, AJM, and, of course, my two sisters.

First US edition 2023
First published by HarperCollins Children's Books (UK) 2022

Library of Congress Catalog Card Number 2022915225
ISBN 978-1-5362-3112-0

22 23 24 25 26 27 28 APS 10 9 8 7 6 5 4 3 2 1

Printed in Humen, Dongguan, China

This book was typeset in Bembo.

Candlewick Press
99 Dover Street
Somerville, Massachusetts 02144

www.candlewick.com

Thanks to Hachette Children's Books for use of the Clarice Bean series lettering